The Fantastic
Dinosaur Adventure

The Fantastic Dinosaur Adventure

by GERALD DURRELL

illustrated by Graham Percy

SIMON AND SCHUSTER BOOKS FOR YOUNG READERS
Published by Simon & Schuster Inc., New York

This book (by kind permission from a committee of three)
is again for Samantha, Genevieve *and* Olivia,
with love from
GERRY PA

This book belongs to

Thanks are due to Dr. Michael Benton, Department of Geology,
Queens University of Belfast, for his invaluable advice.

SIMON AND SCHUSTER BOOKS FOR YOUNG READERS
Simon & Schuster Building, Rockefeller Center
1230 Avenue of the Americas, New York, New York 10020

10 9 8 7 6 5 4 3 2 1

Library of Congress Cataloging-in-Publication Data

Durrell, Gerald Malcolm, 1925-   The fantastic dinosaur adventure / by Gerald Durrell;
illustrated by Graham Percy. Summary: Three children travel back through time in their great
uncle's time machine, intending to rescue baby dinosaurs from evil villains. [1. Dinosaurs—
Fiction. 2. Space and time—Fiction.] I. Percy, Graham, ill. II. Title.
PZ7.D9343Fa1 1990 [Fic]—dc20 89-49099 CIP AC
ISBN 0-671-70871-6

Contents

CHAPTER ONE

LANCELOT RETURNS

The Dollybutt children liked what they called a "proper winter," one with clear, blue skies and sunshine, and plenty of clean, white snow that squeaked like mice when they walked on it. Then they could do all their favorite things—snowballing, skating and tobogganing. This particular winter was a truly proper one and the three of them had just spent a happy morning playing in the woods and fields.

Emma had brought a bag of cake crumbs and some nuts. She fed the squirrels, mice and birds who were finding it hard to get food in the empty woods. While she was doing that, the twins, Ivan and Conrad, built a snow fort which they took turns to attack and defend with snowballs. It was very hard work, so they were both glad to rest after an hour or so, while they all drank the hot cocoa and ate the sandwiches they had brought along.

In the afternoon, as they made their way home, the three children stopped at the Middlemasting village pond where they skated round and round until they were quite dizzy.

By teatime a stiff wind had sprung up, the skies had darkened and it had started to snow heavily. The children made their way back to the cottage where their mother, Mrs. Dollybutt, had prepared a delicious spread. When they had finished eating, they sat around the glowing fire, roasting chestnuts in the embers. As usual, they started to talk about the amazing adventure they had been on two years before with their Great-Uncle Lancelot.

"What did you like best about it?" asked Conrad.

"I know what *I* liked best," said Emma, her mouth full of chestnut. "I liked the powder that Lancelot sprinkled over us so we could talk to the animals. That was terrific, to be able to talk to everything from gorillas to whales. No one else in the world has ever had a chance like that, I'll bet."

"I liked the way Belladonna was built. Lancelot certainly knew how to plan things. He thought of everything. Do you remember how he used fireflies as night-lights?" asked Ivan.

Soon they were all chattering happily about their fantastic flying journey around the world. They had gone in a remarkable flying machine called Belladonna—a huge balloon which had a whole house made out of bamboo hanging beneath it.

"It was all wonderful," sighed Emma. "I do miss Belladonna so. I wonder where Lancelot is now?"

"Off somewhere having a wonderful adventure, I'm sure," snorted Ivan. "And not giving so much as a thought to his poor niece and nephews!"

"Hush, shut up a minute. What was that?" said Conrad, holding up his hand.

"What was what?" asked Ivan, looking around, puzzled.

"I thought I heard somebody shouting," said Conrad. "Be quiet and listen a moment."

They fell silent. At first the only sound they could hear was the wind whistling in the thatch of the cottage. Then they all heard a faint voice crying out in the darkness.

"Help! Help! Somebody help me. Help! Help!"

"Quick, someone's in trouble," said Conrad, springing to his feet. "Let's get our coats. Ivan, you fetch the flashlights."

Bundled up against the cold, and each armed with a big flashlight, they opened the front door. A gust of cold wind blew a cloud of snowflakes into the hall. They braved their way outside and stood in the deep snow, listening. Presently they heard the call for help again.

"I think it's coming from over there," said Emma, pointing to the edge of the wood. "Come on, quickly."

They struggled through the snow, helping each other whenever one of them blundered into a snowdrift. At the edge of the wood, they stopped and listened once more. They could hear nothing except the wind in the trees.

"Shout again so we can find you," yelled Ivan, and from quite close by came a deep, roaring reply.

"Help! Help! I'm here, stuck in the ditch," called the voice.

The children moved forward and shone their flashlights into the ditch. There, struggling about in the water and ice, was a great, round, snow-covered form.

"It's a snowman!" exclaimed Emma, in amazement.

"Nonsense!" said Ivan, nervously. "Snowmen don't come to life."

"But it does look like a very fat snowman," insisted Conrad.

"You silly children," boomed the snowman. "Are you just going to stand there all night discussing what I am, while I freeze to death?

I'm not a snowman, can't you see that? You silly, empty-headed . . ."

"There's only one person who carries on like that," squeaked Emma, delightedly. "It must be Great-Uncle Lancelot!"

"Great-Uncle Lancelot?" cried the twins together. "What's he doing in that ditch?"

"Having a hot bath, can't you see?" snorted Lancelot, for indeed it was he, as large as life and looking extremely cold. "Don't ask silly questions, just get me out of here!"

So they pulled and heaved and panted and gasped until, finally, Lancelot slid out of the ditch and lay exhausted on the snow-covered ground, puffing and blowing like a beached elephant seal.

As soon as the children got Lancelot back to the cottage, Mrs. Dollybutt bustled around like a mother hen. She told him to take off his wet clothes, wrapped him in blankets and made him sit with his feet in a tin basin full of hot water.

When the family saw Lancelot in the light, they were horrified to see that he had a black eye and a swollen, bloody nose.

"What *have* you been doing to yourself?" cried Mrs. Dollybutt.

"I didn't do anything to myself, it was done to me," growled Lancelot, sipping hot soup. "It's a long story."

The children and Mrs. Dollybutt all clustered around the fire, eager to hear Lancelot's tale.

"As you know," he began, proudly stroking his walrus mustache, "I'm a bit of an inventor—in fact, quite a brilliant inventor, although I don't like to boast. During the past year, I've been experimenting with a machine that could transport me back in time."

"What a wonderful idea!" exclaimed Emma. "Did it work?"

"It did," replied Lancelot, "and the test trials were perfect. I went back to the Battle of Trafalgar and had a few words with Nelson. Then I went to the Battle of Waterloo and saw Napoleon's defeat. It was a treat, I can tell you. Just imagine, the very first machine which allows human beings to move back and forth in time. My time machine is the most important invention of this century, or any other century, come to that."

"Where is it?" asked Ivan, eagerly. "Did you bring it with you?"

"No," replied Lancelot, gloomily. "For the simple reason that it's been stolen."

"Stolen!" exclaimed Emma. "How awful! Who stole it?"

"The wickedest men in England," said Lancelot. "Sir Jasper Collywobble and his awful henchman, Throttlethumbs."

"Who are *they?*" asked Ivan.

"Sir Jasper is a famous big-game hunter," replied Lancelot. "He travels all over the world looking for animals to shoot—the bigger the better. Throttlethumbs, his bodyguard, helps him."

"How ghastly," Ivan gasped, horrified.

"How horrible," added Emma, deeply shocked.

"But why would Sir Jasper want your time machine?" asked Conrad.

"He's after the biggest game of all," replied Lancelot, emphatically. "Dinosaurs!"

There was a long silence. The children looked at each other while they digested this news.

"How do you know all this?" asked Conrad, at last.

"I have a time-tracker which can trace my time machine," explained Lancelot, "and with it I discovered that Sir Jasper has traveled back to the Age of Dinosaurs—the Triassic period, to be precise. The rest I had to guess, but I'm sure he has gone hunting for dinosaurs to add to his collection of trophies. But even worse, he'll certainly try to capture some baby dinosaurs to bring back to the present. He could sell them to circuses and safari parks and make a fortune."

Lancelot took two photographs from his wallet and showed them to the children.

"Here," he said. "This is what the two villains look like."

The children shuddered as they looked at the photographs.

"Ugh! Sir Jasper has eyes like a snake," muttered Ivan, looking at the cold, expressionless face.

"And Throttlethumbs looks like a gorilla," said Conrad, pointing to the twisted, blackened teeth and bristly hair.

"They're not a pretty pair," agreed Lancelot. "Throttlethumbs used to be a professional wrestler. That's how he got his strange name. It's what he called himself in the wrestling ring. They say he can crack a coconut with his bare hands. Well, he certainly tried to crack me open when I caught him breaking into my workshop last night. I gave him nearly as good as I got, but I couldn't stop him from stealing my time machine."

"Why, that explains your black eye," said Emma.

"Exactly. And this," continued Lancelot, showing them a third photograph, "is Sir Jasper's balloon, the Jezabella."

"How sinister she looks," commented Emma. "Not at all like our beautiful Belladonna."

"Can't you report Sir Jasper to the police?" asked Conrad.

"Yes, and get him and his accomplice locked up," agreed Ivan.

"You must do something. You can't take this lying down," said Emma.

Lancelot looked around anxiously, as if fearing there might be

eavesdroppers. Then he winked at the children and leaned forward.

"I've got a secret," he explained, in a hoarse whisper.

"What?" the children asked, eagerly.

"Well, when Throttlethumbs knocked me unconscious and stole the time machine, he also took what he must have thought were the blueprints. He was wrong. What he actually stole was a set of plans for a slimming machine I'm inventing. I've still got the plans for the time machine, so I can build another one whenever I want!"

"Wonderful," cried Emma, enthusiastically. "You *are* lucky."

"Ah, but there's much more than that," continued Lancelot, in a conspiratorial tone. "You see, the time machine can take Sir Jasper back in time as easy as pie. It's a very simple machine and he'll soon learn how to use it. But what he doesn't know is that there's a vital part missing."

"Missing? What's missing?" asked Conrad.

"The Gizmo!" chortled Lancelot, triumphantly. "It's the most important part. The machine can easily travel in time, but it's not powerful enough to return to the present day without the Gizmo."

"Why not?" chorused the twins.

"Hopping about in time uses up a lot of power," explained Lancelot, searching for simple words to explain something which was obviously very complicated. "The Gizmo is a booster which provides the extra . . . er . . . ooomph . . . to push the time machine through the time barrier back to the twentieth century."

The children looked at each other with puzzled frowns.

"You mean, without the Gizmo, Sir Jasper is trapped in the Age of the Dinosaurs," said Conrad, slowly understanding the importance of Lancelot's explanation.

"Precisely," replied Lancelot.

"That'll teach him. He'll have to spend the rest of his life with the dinosaurs. I hope they tear him into little pieces," cried Ivan.

"It'll serve him right," added Emma.

"Ah, but you've forgotten why he's gone there," said Lancelot.

"He's probably catching baby dinosaurs at this very moment, and the only way he can do that is to shoot their mothers first."

"But he can't get them back here," Conrad pointed out.

"I know," agreed Lancelot, "but *he* doesn't know that yet. Any number of unfortunate dinosaurs may be killed before he finds out."

"We've simply got to stop him, the cruel beast!" cried Emma.

"I hoped you'd say that," smiled Lancelot. "That's why I came to see you, to get your help. I would have been here hours ago but I had to land because of the snowstorm and then I got lost and fell into that wretched ditch. Now, listen, all of you. I can build another time machine in about two weeks. We can then use my time-tracker to follow Sir Jasper and put an end to his foul plans. We have the Gizmo, so we'll be able to get back to the present all right."

"What a wonderful idea!" cheered Conrad.

"What an adventure!" cried Ivan.

"What will Mother say?" muttered Emma, to herself.

They never did hear what Mrs. Dollybutt had to say because they were packed off to bed. Emma lay awake, listening to the faint sound of Lancelot and her mother arguing in the kitchen below. After what seemed like hours, she heard the stairs creaking as Lancelot climbed them on his way to bed. She listened as he stopped on the landing.

"It's all right. She's agreed!" Lancelot announced, in a loud stage whisper. "I've persuaded her that the rescue of the dinosaurs and the foiling of Sir Jasper's wicked plans are absolutely vital and that, of course, I can't do it without your help. So you'll be coming too."

Emma heard the twins give a quiet cheer. Then she turned over and, tired out by the day's excitement, went straight to sleep.

The next day the children went with Lancelot into the woods to where he had tethered Belladonna. Their hearts filled with joy as they saw her fat, friendly form through the trees. When they got nearer, they stopped and stared in astonishment, for floating alongside Belladonna, tied to her by a silken rope, was a tiny balloon.

"Gosh! Has Belladonna had a baby?" asked Emma, in amazement.

"Not quite," Lancelot laughed. "Let me introduce you to Minidonna. I found the Gizmo didn't work if it was too close to the time machine, so I built Minidonna to carry it. Now, let's get on board, and you can see if things are still as you remember them."

The children ran about Belladonna, saying hello to the animals.

"The electricity is still supplied by the electric eels, I see," observed Conrad, peering into their tank.

"And the South American spiders are still spinning the silk for the balloon and all the ropes," called Emma.

"Let's have an apple," shouted Ivan, running into the garden. He raced through the rows of vegetables and into the solar-heated greenhouses looking for fruit.

The children dashed backward and forward through the flying home, shouting with excitement, "Do you remember this?" or "Do you remember that?" They explored the bedrooms, the bathrooms, the living room, the kitchen and the pantry. They finished up on the flight deck. Here they inspected the solar-powered engine and looked through the telescopes.

Eventually, when they had all calmed down, Lancelot started the engine. They hauled up the anchor ropes and Belladonna, with Minidonna sailing along behind, made a short hop to the field behind the cottage. Lancelot landed the two balloons next to the large barn which stood there.

"The barn will be our workshop," he announced. "Now, let's get to work."

Piles of strange equipment arrived regularly from London, and Lancelot worked from dawn to dusk building the time machine. Conrad, who found the whole business fascinating, helped him.

Ivan and Emma, meanwhile, spring-cleaned Belladonna from top to bottom. They painted the bits of bamboo that needed it, beat the carpets, washed the curtains and made sure that the stores were all in order. They filled the pantry and kitchen cupboards with canned goods such as sardines, salmon, crab and corned beef. They loaded sacks of rice, lentils and barley into the storerooms.

The great day came when Lancelot and Conrad, looking very proud of themselves, announced that their job was done. Time machine Mark II was ready. It was a very strange contraption indeed, with dozens of wheels, tubes, wires and lights. To Emma and Ivan it looked like a lot of scrap iron welded together. They doubted that it would work but they did not say so, as Lancelot and Conrad obviously had great faith in it.

The children said a tearful farewell to Mrs. Dollybutt and climbed on board Belladonna. Lancelot sprinkled each of them with his special powder that would allow them to talk to the dinosaurs when they reached their destination. Then he spread out three large maps on the table on the flight deck.

"What are those?" asked Ivan, curiously.

"Maps of the world," replied Lancelot.

"Which world? They don't look a bit like the maps in our atlases," said Emma, bending over the table and examining the maps more closely.

"Of course not," laughed Lancelot. "These are maps of the world as it looked millions of years ago. This one shows the world in the Triassic period. In those days there were no separate continents, just one huge one called Pangaea. The northern half of Pangaea is called Laurasia and the southern part is called Gondwanaland."

The children stared, fascinated. Lancelot pointed to a huge ocean which nearly cut Pangaea in half.

"That ocean is called Tethys," he continued. "All that's left of it nowadays is the Mediterranean Sea. Now, this second map shows the world in the Jurassic period. You can see that the continents have all drifted apart. This third map shows the world in the Cretaceous period, and you can see the continents are starting to join up again. It almost looks like the world today."

"How fascinating," said Conrad. "You mean the world was changing as well as the animals?"

"Of course," said Lancelot. Then he pointed to a spot on Pangaea. "Now, according to the time-tracker, this is where Sir Jasper has gone. It's not far from here in miles but it's nearly two hundred and ten million years away in time. Strap yourselves carefully into those seats and don't do anything until I tell you."

He went to where the time machine stood in a corner of the flight deck and pulled a lot of knobs. Then, when he pressed a button, red and purple lights started flashing. Lancelot rushed to his own seat and strapped himself in. The children felt Belladonna shuddering and twitching as though she was alive. Then the lights grew dim.

"We're off!" shouted Lancelot. "Dinosaurs, here we come!"

Strange things began to happen. Colored lights flashed over them—green, blue, yellow and red. One minute, it was extremely hot and the next, extremely cold. The air was filled with strange sounds—twangings, bangings, whooshings and whines. Finally, there was a great BANG, followed by a flood of sunlight. Lancelot struggled out of his seat and rushed onto the flight deck.

"Come on!" he called, excitedly. "We're here! Welcome to the Triassic period—the dawn of the Age of the Dinosaurs."

CHAPTER TWO
THROUGH THE TIME BARRIER

The children ran out to the rail of the flight deck and looked around. Stretching away into the distance, under the cloudless sky which was as blue as a cornflower, was a rolling desert of sand dunes, while immediately below them was a great swamp. These two areas were separated by huge stone outcrops of brick-red rock and a large forest. Belladonna dropped closer to the ground, passing over several volcanoes. These looked like cone-shaped chimneys, each with a wisp of smoke curling from its top. As they swooped over the forest and swamp they spotted a few trees which looked vaguely familiar, although there were many others they did not recognize. The lovely shades of green, flecked here and there with scarlet and gold, hinted that it was the beginning of autumn.

"Phew! Isn't it hot?" gasped Ivan, taking off his sweater. The others followed suit.

"Oh, look," cried Emma, in surprise. "Aren't those monkey-puzzle trees?"

"Yes," replied Lancelot. "They're ancestors of the monkey-puzzle trees we have in our gardens today. Look over there. You see that glade of huge trees? They're ginkgos. We'd only seen them as fossils and then, recently, some were found growing in China."

"You mean they survived the dinosaurs?" asked Conrad.

"Oh, yes. A lot of plants and animals did," replied Lancelot.

"Well, what I want to know is, where are the dinosaurs?" asked Ivan, impatiently. "I don't see a single one."

"You will," Lancelot reassured him. "We're still quite high up."

Slowly, Belladonna dropped down lower until the bamboo house was almost brushing the treetops. Soon they were flying over the great swamp. The trees growing out of the water were very curious. They had thick, jointed trunks, like huge bamboo stalks, with leaves that looked like long pine needles growing from each joint.

"Why," commented Emma, "they're like giant versions of the horsetails that grow around the pond in Middlemasting."

"That's exactly what they are," nodded Lancelot. Then he pointed down. "I say, look over there, isn't that a fine sight?"

The children saw dozens of huge dragonflies flicking and gliding between the trunks of the horsetails. Their iridescent bodies and transparent wings glittered like rainbows in the sunlight.

"Gosh! They're as big as kestrels," gasped Ivan. "How amazing!"

"Look, there—crocodiles!" shouted Conrad, in excitement.

Lying on the banks of the swamp were strange, crocodilelike creatures which, as soon as Belladonna's shadow fell over them, slithered down into the green murky waters.

They flew on, fascinated by their first glimpse of the strange world in which they had arrived. They saw green and gold lizards gliding from tree to tree, supported on wings of skin stiffened by their extra-long ribs. Then, as they rounded a clump of tall ginkgos, they saw their first dinosaurs.

Browsing in the shallow waters were a group of long-necked plateosaurs. There were two babies, and three adults which were about the size of elephants. They kept dipping their heads and long necks into the water and munching great mouthfuls of waterweeds. They made gurgling, moaning noises to each other as they browsed contentedly. Occasionally, one would rear up on its hind legs to pluck a branch from a tree, and the children were amazed to see that it could stand almost as high as a house.

"They look as tame as a herd of cows," commented Emma, watching them through the telescope.

"They are," replied Lancelot. "Not all dinosaurs are terrible monsters, you know. That's just rubbish you read in comics and see in films."

They had been so busy watching the plateosaurs, none of them had noticed that a stiff wind had sprung up. Belladonna, left to her own devices, was now bowling along at an alarming rate, clearing the trees and leaving the swamp behind. Before they could collect their thoughts, they found they were heading straight toward a massive outcrop of red rocks.

Lancelot made a dive for the engine, but too late! There was a crash as the bamboo house struck the rocks, followed by a grinding, squeaking sound. It was dragged along and then came to a halt between two rock pillars, which stood up like huge chimney stacks. The shock of the impact threw them all into a tangled heap of arms and legs.

"We're stuck," cried Lancelot, struggling to his feet and looking over the rail. "You children get out and start pushing. I'll put the engine into reverse and then join you."

The children felt a bit queer as they stepped out of the front door into what was, after all, dinosaur land. But except for plants, there was not a living thing to be seen. They pushed and they shoved at the bamboo house. Soon, Lancelot joined them. They huffed and they puffed, but it was useless. Belladonna was well and truly trapped between the rocks.

They were leaning against the house, panting and wiping the sweat from their brows, when Emma gave a faint scream and pointed. Turning, they saw a group of strange reptiles coming swiftly down the slope toward them. The creatures ran with their backs parallel to the ground, carrying their long tails stretched out behind them. Their mouths were full of extremely sharp-looking teeth and they were all chanting in shrill, hissing voices, "Food, food, we must have food!" and, "Delicious food, we must have food!"

"Don't panic," shouted Lancelot. "They're Coelophysis. They're meat-eaters, but remember we can talk to them. Still, you children had better get inside, just in case."

The children did as they were told, while Lancelot stood his ground, facing the Coelophysis, who were now gnashing their teeth as well as chanting to each other, "I'll have the fat one."

"No, *I'll* have the fat one!"

"Oh, delicious arms and legs! We'll eat them all, every scrap."

"Now, look here, we're friends. Strangers in your country. We mean no harm, we're just travelers," shouted Lancelot.

"Not travelers—food," hissed the nearest Coelophysis, thrusting its mouth, which was full of dreadful teeth, at Lancelot.

Lancelot leaped to one side. The Coelophysis hissed with rage as it banged its nose on the side of the house. As Lancelot scrambled hastily inside, the twins slammed and bolted the door behind him.

Immediately, the front door began to shudder and shake as the Coelophysis attacked it. They bit long splinters out of the bamboo, hissing, "Food—food—come out and be devoured."

"Quick, to the flight deck," shouted Lancelot. "I'll try to talk some sense into them before they do any more damage."

Once on the flight deck, Lancelot seized the bullhorn.

"Now look here, you silly creatures," he shouted, "stop behaving stupidly, and talk."

The Coelophysis looked up at him. They gnashed their teeth and hissed, "Fat, fabulous food, come down."

Then they went back to the business of breaking down the front door.

Just as the children were wondering what on earth they could do to save themselves, there was an enormous, rumbling WHOOSH which made Belladonna shake violently.

The rocks which trapped them were on the slopes of a small volcano which had started to erupt. There was a loud roar. A huge cloud, like a black-and-white cauliflower, burst from the top of the volcano and ashes rained down on them.

The ground shuddered violently and one of the huge rocks that wedged them was dislodged. It slid to one side, releasing Belladonna. Immediately, the balloon floated upward in a cloud of cinders and ash. They were safe! Far below them, the children could see a great river of fiery lava which engulfed the Coelophysis and in a moment burned them to a cinder.

"Phew!" exclaimed Lancelot, mopping his brow with a purple-and-green handkerchief. "What a narrow escape!"

"I thought you said all that stuff about dinosaurs being fierce was nonsense," protested Ivan, indignantly.

"Yes," agreed Emma. "You said . . ."

"I don't care what I said!" roared Lancelot. "Now, stop bothering me and let's go and look for a safe campsite, for heaven's sake. I can't stand children who chatter all the time."

As they floated away, the volcano continued to explode, pushing its great, cauliflower-shaped cloud into the sky and raining down ashes and red-hot pumice stone. Lancelot and the children busied themselves with brushes and pans, sweeping the flight deck clear and dumping the deadly debris over the side to stop the bamboo house from catching fire.

Suddenly, Lancelot started to shout and dance about, tearing his hair. The children almost jumped out of their skins.

"Oh, woe and agony!" he yelled, running about the flight deck in a great panic. "Oh, woe!"

"What on earth's the matter?" gasped Conrad.

"Have you burned yourself?" asked Emma.

"No, it's much worse than that. Look!" roared Lancelot, pointing upward with a dramatic gesture.

They looked up and saw, to their dismay, that a piece of glowing, red-hot pumice stone had fallen on the balloon. It was caught in one of the ropes and was burning a hole in the silk. There was nothing they could do. As the hole got bigger, the balloon started to collapse. Slowly Belladonna sank lower and lower.

"Quick!" bellowed Lancelot. "We must find a safe landing spot." He rushed to a telescope and surveyed the countryside below.

"Over there," he shouted. "The little group of trees by that pool in the sand dunes is perfect. We can hide Belladonna and there's open ground all around so we can see any dinosaurs coming."

29

They only just made it, for Belladonna had practically no air left in her. They bumped onto the sandy earth near the little wood and beside a large pool over which hung a sort of mist. As soon as they landed, they seized buckets and rushed out to the pool to get water to put out the fire.

"Why," cried Emma, in astonishment, as they filled their buckets, "the water's hot, and this is steam rising from it, not mist."

"It's a volcanic hot spring," explained Lancelot. "Very useful. We'll all be able to have a nice swim presently, but let's save Belladonna first or we'll never get back home safely."

Eventually, they did put out the fire, but by then the balloon had a hole in it the size of a tabletop. The twins sat down to rest, while Emma picked up the piece of pumice stone which had caused the fire as a souvenir. Lancelot went to set the spiders to work spinning a large patch of silk to repair the hole.

"Let's have a swim," suggested Ivan. "I'm covered with ash."

"Oh, yes! That would be lovely," agreed Emma. "My hair is so full of volcanic dust that it feels like a helmet."

"It looks like one too," laughed Conrad.

Lancelot joined them and they all splashed about happily. The pool was deliciously warm and, apart from a few tiny, green, shrimplike animals, free from any form of life.

Several trees fringed the pool. On their branches, the children found a host of tiny, fragile, lizardlike creatures with fingerlike projections on their backs. They changed color like chameleons. One minute they matched the green leaves, the next they turned gray as they crawled into the shadows. They even turned

brilliant scarlet when they crawled over to feed on bunches of the bright berries. They were very beautiful. Emma thought they looked like living Christmas tree decorations. They tried talking to them, but the reptiles had such faint, tinkling voices that the children could not understand them.

Huge, green dragonflies with red eyes hawked over the pool. One of them suddenly zoomed at an unsuspecting crested lizard and seized it. Ivan windmilled his arms through the water, sending a cascade of spray over the dragonfly. It dropped the lizard and glided away, muttering angrily to itself. The little lizards seemed delighted and crawled over Ivan, presumably thanking him, though their voices were so faint that it was impossible to tell.

"Well," announced Lancelot, as they finished their swim, "it's my turn to cook today, so I'd better get started. While I'm getting the meal, why don't you go off and look for Jasper's campsite? The time-tracker shows that it can't be far away."

"Perhaps he's been eaten by a Coelophysis," grinned Ivan. "It would serve Sir Jasper right, but he might give the poor dinosaur a terrible dose of the collywobbles!"

"Listen carefully," continued Lancelot, ignoring the laughter which greeted this awful joke. "Use your pedometers to work out when you've traveled exactly a mile in a straight line from here. Then use your compasses to walk in a circle searching for those villains. But keep out of sight. They don't yet know that we're after them, and if we can surprise them it'll be to our advantage."

"What about the wildlife around here?" asked Conrad.

"Well, all I can say is, take great care," warned Lancelot. "You'll find the vegetarians quite harmless, but you'll have to watch out for the meat-eaters. As you saw just now, they can turn quite nasty, but I think I can rely on you to behave in a sensible manner. Now, off you go and don't take any risks."

Once they had changed, the children set off, armed with notebooks, cameras and binoculars. Before long, they reached a swampy forest of giant horsetails. They made their way through the great trees until they reached the edge of a swamp. Here they found a herd of plateosaurs feeding on the lush waterweeds. Alongside floated a group of tubby creatures with Dracula-like front teeth.

"Those are Placerias," said Conrad, who had been carefully studying a big book on dinosaurs. "They behave more like hippos than anything else. They seem to get on all right with the plateosaurs, don't they?"

"What are those dinosaurs on the bank?" whispered Emma. "They look a bit like chickens."

"Procompsognathi," Conrad replied.

Five of the creatures were moving cautiously through the undergrowth, making frequent pauses and looking from left to right. They reached the water's edge and started to drink.

"Are those logs drifting in the water?" asked Emma, pointing.

"No," Conrad whispered excitedly, focusing the binoculars. "They're not logs. They're phytosaurs. They're like crocodiles. See how they're drifting toward the procompsognathi. I think they're going to attack!"

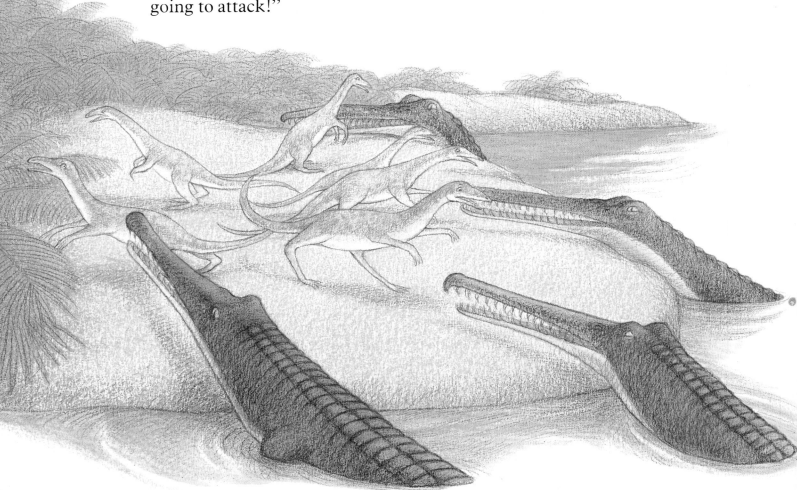

The children watched breathlessly as the phytosaurs floated slowly toward the procompsognathi who were drinking, completely unaware of the danger. The phytosaurs drifted closer and closer and then made a great commotion in the water as they splashed everywhere. The terrified procompsognathi turned to run, but it was too late!

The ferocious phytosaurs were among them, their mouths snapping and their tails whipping to and fro. They seized the procompsognathi in their huge jaws, threw back their heads and scrunched them up.

The spurting blood and screams of the dying dinosaurs were so ghastly that the children closed their eyes and covered their ears. At last, to their relief, the fight ended. Carrying the limp bodies of their prey back into the water, the phytosaurs sank from sight.

"Ugh! That was worse than my worst nightmare," shivered Ivan, looking pale. "And just think, it could have been one of us!"

"Don't say that," protested Emma, shuddering. "Can we go now please, before anything else horrible happens?"

After walking for an hour or so, they came to a canyon which cut deep into high cliffs. Once inside the steep walls, they were in deep, cool shadows. Near the far end they saw long, shrewlike creatures scuttling in and out of the rocks.

"Look!" whispered Conrad, highly excited. "Those are the first mammals. All modern mammals have evolved from them."

"They're such tiny and insignificant little animals, like mice," breathed Emma. "I can't believe they've evolved into whales."

"Not to mention gorillas or even people," whispered Ivan.

Fascinated, the children watched their mammal ancestors. The creatures' striped silver-and-black fur was a very effective camouflage, for when they sat still among the shadowy rocks, they were almost invisible. Emma and the twins spent a long time trying to tempt them closer, but they were too shy.

"Listen! Can you hear a peculiar noise?" asked Emma, cocking her head and looking toward the end of the canyon.

"I can certainly hear something," replied Conrad. "Let's go and investigate."

33

CHAPTER THREE
TOO CLOSE FOR COMFORT

Emerging from the twilight of the canyon, the children stood blinking in the bright light as they surveyed the scene. In front of them, the canyon had widened into a broad valley with a long, blue lake in the middle.

Flying over the water was a flock of the most extraordinary looking creatures imaginable. They had leathery wings about two yards across which pointed backward, and long, whiplike tails which trailed behind them. They had lizardlike heads and long, pointed beaks full of sharp teeth. Their bodies were covered in thick, brown fur. Every now and then, one of these creatures wheeled and dived into the water with a sharp splash.

"I say, they're diving for huge fish and keeping them in their pouches like pelicans do," remarked Ivan, training the binoculars on them. "What on earth are they?"

"They must be early pterosaurs," replied Conrad. "I'm not sure, but they might be Eudimorphodon."

"Heavens!" exclaimed Emma. "What a name! Imagine trying to introduce one to your friends. You couldn't do it, you'd get too tongue-tied. I think pterosaur is easier."

"Here, give me the binoculars for a second," requested Conrad, peering up at the cliff. "I want to look at something."

He trained the binoculars up the cliff and gave a grunt of surprise.

"Look up there," he said, handing the binoculars to Emma. "There's a whole colony of them."

Emma looked up and saw dozens of baby pterosaurs sitting on the rocky ledges craning their necks, preening themselves, clattering their beaks together and flapping their wings. The children moved closer to take photographs.

The noise was deafening. The baby pterosaurs kept up a constant wheezing and squeaking. This, combined with their flapping wings as well as the clatter of their beaks, made an incredible racket.

"What an awful row!" shouted Ivan, raising his voice above the din. "You'd have to be deaf to live among them."

The children watched in fascination, camera shutters clicking, as three large pterosaurs flew up from the lake, their pouches full of fish. Seeing the approaching adults, the babies grew frantic and the noise increased even more. Awkwardly, the parent pterosaurs clung to the ledges with their hands and feet while they pushed fish into the gaping beaks of their hungry babies.

"Time to move on," said Conrad, eventually. "We'll use up all our film at this rate."

At the end of the valley, the countryside became flatter and thickly studded with trees. They passed occasional hot springs which created drifts of steam with tiny rainbows in them. They had not walked far when they heard groaning noises off to their left, accompanied by ground-shaking thumps and crashes.

"Oh, dear! I hope it's not another volcano," worried Emma.

"No, I don't think so," Conrad reassured her. "It sounds more like animals."

"Friendly ones, I hope," muttered Ivan.

They crept forward cautiously and in a clearing they saw a group of plateosaurs with their babies. They were all moaning and groaning, the tears running down their cheeks as they tried to lift up a plateosaur which was lying on the ground.

"It must be dead," announced Conrad. "They're trying to lift it up, hoping it'll come to life again. Elephants do that when somebody shoots one of their herd."

"This one's been shot too," reported Ivan, grimly, training the binoculars on the dead plateosaur. "I can see three bullet holes."

"Let me look," demanded Conrad, taking the binoculars. "Oh, no! That must be Sir Jasper's work."

"Poor thing," said Emma, shakily. "Shall we go and help?"

"They might think we're with Sir Jasper and attack us," objected Conrad, doubtfully.

"Well, I vote we try," said Ivan. "They are vegetarians and Lancelot did say that vegetarians weren't as fierce as meat-eaters."

"Let's risk it," agreed Emma, standing up. "They might even know where Sir Jasper is."

The children left the trees and walked with thumping hearts across the clearing. The huge animals were so wrapped up in their grief that the children were quite close to them before they were spotted. One of the babies gave a shrill squeak of alarm.

"Forgive us for disturbing you," called Emma toward the towering heads which had turned to stare down at them. "We just wanted to say we're sorry about your friend."

"I don't understand," sobbed one of the beasts. "It was dinosaurs like yourselves who killed my mate and stole my baby."

"Yes, I know," said Conrad, "and we're terribly sorry, but we're here to catch the ones who did it and punish them."

"But what about my baby? They carried her off, you know," said the Plateosaurus, tears as big as plums running down his face and plopping onto the ground.

"Don't worry," said Emma firmly, "we'll get her back."

"How can you?" asked the distraught Plateosaurus. "They flew off over those trees in a round, red-and-black . . ."

"Yes, we know," said Ivan. "A balloon. We've got one that'll travel twice as fast. Now you've told us the direction they've gone, we'll soon pick up their trail. The sooner we get going, the sooner we'll catch up with them. Come on, you two, let's go."

"Good luck," called the Plateosaurus, watching as the children turned and disappeared among the trees.

"If we catch up with Sir Jasper, I'll pull his mustache out by the roots and that's just for starters," stormed Emma, angry tears running down her face.

The twins pushed on grimly through the undergrowth.

"I smell smoke," reported Ivan, a few minutes later. "This way."

Struggling through some thick bushes, they came upon the remains of Sir Jasper's camp in a small clearing. Near the smoldering embers of a fire, they found lots of cans, empty bottles and bits of paper.

"Look at all this rubbish they've left," said Emma, looking around at the mess. "It's bad enough littering up our own time without coming back to ruin the Triassic."

"And look at that fire," added Conrad, angrily. "Leaving a fire smoldering like that could set the whole countryside ablaze."

"Let's go back. We've got to tell Lancelot we've found Sir Jasper's camp and that he's left," suggested Ivan, and the others agreed.

After traveling for about half an hour they felt thirsty.

"Let's stop over there by those big rocks," suggested Emma. "It'll be nice to be in the shade of those trees."

They sat down by the rocks and drank the lemonade they had brought.

"This has all been terrifically exciting," sighed Emma, contentedly, leaning against a rock, "but will we ever catch up with Sir Jasper and that awful Throttlethumbs?"

"I bet they've caught all they want here and have moved on to the next age," said Ivan. "What's it called, Conrad?"

"The Jurassic," Conrad replied, "but my guess is that they're anxious to get to the Cretaceous period."

"Why?" asked Emma.

"Because that's the age with the most spectacular dinosaurs in it," answered Conrad. "You know, really big, fierce ones."

"Well, I think some of them are quite fierce enough here," said Emma firmly. "I've never been so frightened in my life."

"Has everyone finished?" asked Conrad. "We ought to move on. We'll never get back at this rate."

They set off and were soon jumping from rock to rock along the edge of a swamp. Emma, distracted by some beautiful dragonflies which flew past, lost her balance and fell into the water. Ivan and Conrad leaned over, grabbed Emma's hands and hauled her back up onto the rocks as quickly as they could.

"Are you all right?" asked Conrad, looking very concerned.

"I think so," said Emma, grimacing, "except that I seem to have sprained my wretched ankle."

"Heavens! Look at those creatures over there!" cried Ivan, forgetting about Emma in his surprise. "What on earth are they?"

Over on the opposite bank stood three huge reptiles, each as big as a bus. Their heads and necks were in the water, swinging to and fro like pendulums.

"They're called Tanystropheus," Conrad informed them loudly, "and I think they're fishing."

Hearing his voice, one of the animals raised its head out of the water. The children gaped with astonishment, for its neck was as tall as a lamppost. Its small, lizardlike head had a mouthful of sharp-looking teeth, with which it was chewing a big fish. It saw the children, swallowed the fish and screeched like someone playing the bagpipes. Immediately, the other two reptiles lifted their heads out of the water and stared at the children as well. The next moment all three of them waddled into the water and started swimming toward Emma and the twins.

"They're coming after us!" exclaimed Ivan. "Run for it."

"I can't run with this ankle," wailed Emma, in panic.

"I'll carry you," suggested Conrad. "Quick! Hop on my back."

They set off as fast as they could, with Emma riding piggyback on Conrad, while Ivan brought up the rear.

"Go for the . . . trees," panted Conrad, ". . . climb out of reach."

"They're right behind us," puffed Ivan. "Get a move on!"

"Up here," gasped Conrad, stopping by a very tall ginkgo.

Emma, terror overcoming the pain in her ankle, climbed swiftly, closely followed by the twins. A few seconds later, one of their pursuers arrived at the bottom of the tree and, reaching out, seized Ivan's jacket in its jaws. Ivan clung on for dear life while the reptile tried to pull him down.

"Take your coat off, quick!" panted Emma. "Here, I'll help you."

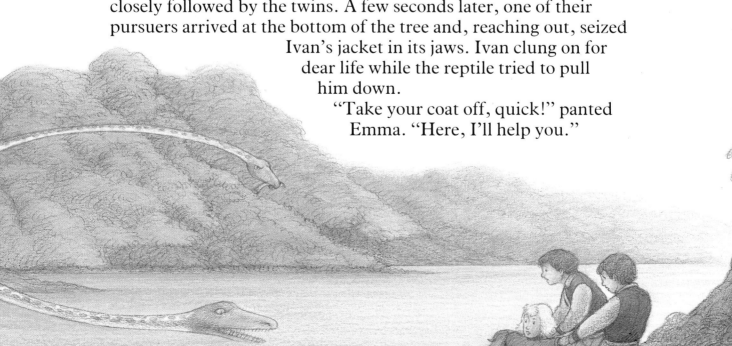

Ivan's strength was fading fast as Emma, thinking at lightning speed, drew her knife, reached down and slashed his coat in two. The reptile paused to chew on the material, thinking it was Ivan.

"Now, quick!" gasped Emma. "Before it realizes. Climb!"

They climbed as they had never climbed before, and reached the top. They were safe for the moment although shaking with exhaustion and fear. Below, the reptiles snarled with rage, then started banging the trunk. The horrified children soon realized that the tree, which was rooted in soft, marshy ground, was starting to tilt. The top began to lean toward the swamp, threatening to tip them into the water where they would be easy prey for the reptiles.

"I wish we'd never come on this adventure," sobbed Emma, her teeth chattering with fright.

"It's all right," croaked Conrad, hoarsely. "Look up there!"

Emma and Ivan gasped with relief as they saw Minidonna floating toward them like a soap bubble through the treetops.

"Three cheers for Minidonna!" they shouted, waving furiously.

"Did you have a nice time with the long-necks?" grinned Lancelot, as he brought Minidonna alongside their shaky perch. "When you didn't return, I went up in Minidonna and spotted you with the telescope. It looks as if I was just in time too."

"It's a wonder my hair hasn't turned snow-white," said Emma, as she scrambled aboard, closely followed by the twins.

"What's for dinner?" asked Ivan, who never forgot about his stomach for long. "I could eat a dinosaur, I'm so hungry."

"Better to eat one than be eaten by one," laughed Lancelot.

As they flew back, Emma told Lancelot their news.

". . . and so you see," she finished, "Sir Jasper's been and gone already, and it's just as you thought, he *is* killing dinosaurs and capturing their babies."

As soon as they reached Belladonna, Lancelot went to the flight deck and turned on the time-tracker.

"You're right," he announced, grimly watching the blip on the screen. "Sir Jasper *has* moved forward to the Jurassic period. Luckily, Belladonna is now fully repaired, so we may be able to catch him before he does any more harm. We'll leave first thing tomorrow morning."

CHAPTER FOUR

PARTING OF THE WAYS

Their flight into the Jurassic was smooth and uneventful. When they unstrapped themselves, they saw that Belladonna was sailing over a shallow sea. The children, now thoroughly rested and relaxed after their ordeal, hung over the rail of the flight deck, enchanted by the sea life they could see in the clear waters below.

Ammonites wandered about on the sandy bottom, their spiral shells the size of bicycle wheels. A huge school of fish churned the water into foam as it fled from a big group of ichthyosaurs, which looked rather like dolphins. The adults, followed by their newborn babies, leaped in long, elegant curves through the air.

"Just look at them leap," said Conrad, admiringly. "Those fish don't stand a chance."

They sailed on inland, over a series of lakes. In the distance a
volcano squatted, with smoke curling out of its cone like steam from
a boiling kettle. Ivan, who was scanning the scenery through a
telescope, started yelling with excitement.

"Look at those!" he shouted, pointing. "They're gigantic, the
biggest we've seen yet."

Standing in the shallow waters at the edge of a lake were about
forty monstrous reptiles with extremely long necks and even longer
tails. The adults were bigger than houses and longer than railroad
locomotives. Even the babies were the size of buses.

"We're in luck. It's a herd of diplodoci. It's possible they may
have seen Jasper. We'll go and ask them," decided Lancelot.

He steered Belladonna to within hailing distance of the reptiles.
The animals were all standing strangely still, necks up, heads
raised, looking away from Belladonna as if listening.

Lancelot turned off the engine and called to the diplodoci.

"I say, excuse me. We don't want to interrupt in any way . . ."

One of the giant dinosaurs turned its head and looked at him.

"Well, *don't* interrupt," he said. "Can't you see we're busy?"

"What are you busy doing?" asked Ivan, nosily.

"One of our herd is in trouble, but he's too far away for us to help," explained the Diplodocus, "so we're sending him encouraging messages."

"By telepathy?" asked Lancelot.

"Er, possibly," answered the Diplodocus, looking a bit puzzled. "Now, I do wish you'd be quiet, this takes a lot of concentration."

"How far away is the one that's in trouble?" asked Emma.

"Far beyond those trees, where that red glow is," replied the reptile, pointing to the other side of the lake.

"Oh, look! It's a huge forest fire over on the other side of the lake," shouted Ivan, looking through the telescope.

"Hang on, everyone!" warned Lancelot, turning on the engine. "Let's go over there and see if we can do anything to help."

They raced across the lake at full speed, toward the forest
fire. As they got closer, they could see flames leaping high
and roaring through the forest. It was obvious that the
fire had been caused by the glowing lava from a nearby
volcano. Through clouds of smoke, they made out the
dim shape of a baby Diplodocus completely
surrounded by fire.

He was uttering loud, quivering screams for
help, while running round and round in circles,
completely panic-stricken as the flames leaped
toward him. There was not a moment to lose!

They lowered an exceptionally strong rope with a
noose in the end, and a rope ladder alongside it. Lancelot
climbed onto the rope ladder and made his way down, swaying
from side to side. When he was level with the baby Diplodocus, he
shouted through the bullhorn.

"Hey! You there!" he roared. "Come over here."

The baby Diplodocus lumbered over to where Lancelot dangled.

"Now," said Lancelot, "stand on your hind legs, so I can get this
noose under your front legs."

"I can't," he whimpered. "I'm too frightened."

"There's no such word as can't," bellowed Lancelot, as the flames crackled nearer and nearer. "This is no time for hysterics. Now, shut up, stand up and let me get this noose around you."

Throwing the rope like a lasso, Lancelot managed, with some difficulty, to get the noose over the baby's head, down his very long neck and under his front legs. Then he climbed back up the ladder.

"Now, stand still," shouted Lancelot fiercely to the baby, and then ordered the twins to haul away.

The children started the winch and soon raised the baby safely out of the fire. Then Belladonna sailed back across the lake with the dinosaur swinging underneath the house like a giant yo-yo.

The diplodoci were delighted with the rescue.

"That was a most brave and kind thing to do," sobbed the mother Diplodocus, gazing at her baby in relief. "If there's ever anything we can do to help you, please let us know."

"Could I have a souvenir of our meeting?" asked Emma.

"What's a souvenir?" murmured the mother Diplodocus, doubtfully.

"Oh, something to remember you by," explained Emma.

"Well, I'm not sure," replied the mother Diplodocus, "but I've got an addled egg if that's any use to you."

"That would be perfect," cried Emma, clapping her hands with joy.

The egg was as big as a melon and Emma stowed it carefully away so that it would not break.

"Thank you kindly. I don't suppose you've seen another . . . er." Lancelot paused, realizing that the dinosaurs would not understand what a balloon was. ". . . I mean, another pterosaur like this around here, have you?"

"As a matter of fact, I have," said the mother Diplodocus. "It was a different color, though. Another species, I suppose."

"Which way did it go?" asked Lancelot, excitedly.

"Over there toward those mountains," she replied.

Thanking the diplodoci, they were soon airborne and hot on the trail of Sir Jasper. Before long, they spied Jezabella anchored in a clearing below. There was no sign of Sir Jasper or his henchman, but they could see many cages in the camp. These contained baby dinosaurs who were looking through the bars and sobbing loudly.

"He must have a heart of stone to do that to the poor little things," cried Emma, furiously.

"Yes, we must stop him at all costs," declared Lancelot. "Now, here's my plan. We'll land here, where I can keep my eye on Jezabella. You go and do some cautious scouting, and see if you can find out what's become of Sir Jasper and Throttlethumbs."

They landed Belladonna and the children set off through the thick wood, talking in whispers and moving very quietly. They were about halfway across an open, sandy clearing when it happened!

From out of the trees rushed a terrifying creature which towered over them. Its powerful legs were armed with long, sharp claws. Its huge head was split by a grinning mouth crammed with razor-sharp teeth. When it saw them, it roared ferociously.

"Allosaurus!" shouted Conrad. "Scatter! It's our only hope!"

Spurred on by their terror, the children ran off in different directions. They did not stop to look back, but if they had, they would have seen that Conrad had been right. The carnosaur stopped, unable to decide which of them to chase. This gave the children the chance to reach the trees. The Allosaurus stalked around the empty clearing then, frustrated, turned back into the forest the way it had come, snarling with disappointment.

After a while, Conrad and Ivan stumbled into each other.

"I've never run so fast in my life," gasped Ivan. "Where's Emma?"

"I don't know," Conrad frowned. "I do hope she's not lost."

"She can't be far," said Ivan. "Come on, let's look for her; but remember, don't shout. That just seems to attract unwelcome attention. Let's do our usual whistle."

Meanwhile, in another part of the wood, Emma had whistled and whistled until her lips were dry, but there was no response. She came to a little clearing which she surveyed cautiously before stepping out into it. She was careful about attacks from the ground, but she had entirely forgotten about possible attacks from the air. There was a sudden WHOOSH and a flap of wings. Before she had time to cry out, Emma was grabbed by the arm and whirled aloft.

Craning her head, she saw that she had been seized by a female gnathosaur, a large, flying reptile. Her wide, fur-covered wings were beating frantically to support Emma's unexpected weight. Her hands and feet were armed with great, curved claws. The sharp teeth in her long beak were starting to dig into Emma's arm.

"Put me down," shouted Emma, as the creature flapped and glided over the trees. "I'm a friend."

"Can't do that, dearie," the Gnathosaurus mumbled indistinctly, through a mouthful of Emma. "You're food for my babies. I've had a bad morning fishing on the lake, so you'll have to do instead. I must say, you don't smell very nice. But still, if they're hungry enough, my babies will eat anything."

"But I don't want to be eaten,"
protested Emma, fearfully. "If you'll
put me down, I'll explain."

"No time," the creature replied. "My babies
are starving to death. You'll be a nice morsel for them,
dearie. You'll make them grow up big and strong."

"I don't want them to grow up big and strong by eating me,"
yelped Emma, trying to wriggle free.

"Selfishness never did anyone any good," retorted the mother
Gnathosaurus. "Nearly there now."

They approached a huge cliff, on the ledges of which sat
hundreds of baby gnathosaurs, all screaming wheezily. The mother
Gnathosaurus flew to a wide, high ledge, where two babies flapped
their wings and shouted expectantly. She plonked Emma on the
ledge and gave her a push toward the babies with her beak.

"There you are, my darlings," she cooed. "Here's a lovely, hot
lunch for you, you lucky little dears."

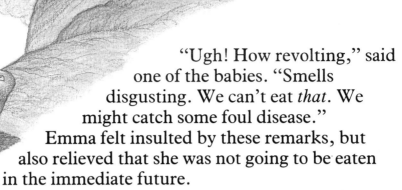

"Ugh! How revolting," said one of the babies. "Smells disgusting. We can't eat *that*. We might catch some foul disease."

Emma felt insulted by these remarks, but also relieved that she was not going to be eaten in the immediate future.

"There's no pleasing you children," sighed their mother, shuffling her wings in irritation. "What *do* you want?"

"Octopus," shouted the babies, "with lots of wriggly tentacles."

"I'll see what I can do," groaned the mother Gnathosaurus and, so saying, she launched herself into the air and flew away, leaving Emma marooned on the ledge with the babies.

"What about me? I can't get down," shouted Emma, despairingly, after her.

"Why, it talks!" said one of the baby gnathosaurs, surprised.

"Of course I do. I'm not a fish," snapped Emma. "I'm a human being. I come from . . . er . . . I come from . . . um . . . far away."

"Far Away, what fun!" the baby said, dreamily. "I've always wanted to go Far Away from this smelly ledge."

"Could you carry me down to the ground?" asked Emma, hopefully.

"Oh, no, I couldn't do that without a good lunch inside me," he replied. "Tell me more about Far Away. Do they have octopus there?"

Emma racked her brains for a way to escape, while the baby Gnathosaurus asked her endless questions about Far Away, which he obviously thought was a country. She had just decided that she would be trapped in the nest forever, when she heard a loud, thumping noise below.

She peered cautiously over the edge. A familiar herd was feeding noisily on succulent, green leaves at the base of the cliff. It was the diplodoci they had met earlier.

"I say, you there, Diplodocus. Please help me," she called.

The Diplodocus herd wheeled about in confusion and looked around for the danger.

"I'm up here," Emma called down. "I need help."

"Oh, it's you," said one of them, looking up and recognizing her.

"Please help me," pleaded Emma. "I want to get down."

"Can't you fly down?" asked the Diplodocus, in a puzzled voice. "You must have flown up there. Why not fly down the same way?"

"I didn't fly up here, I was carried," replied Emma, indignantly. "Can you get me down and take me back to my balloon?"

"What's a balloon?" inquired the baby Gnathosaurus.

"Funny, that's what *I* was going to ask," said the Diplodocus.

"Well, what *is* a balloon?" asked the baby Gnathosaurus.

"Dunno," replied the Diplodocus. "That's why I nearly asked."

"What carryings-on!" thought Emma. "No wonder they became extinct!"

"It's our flying machine. You saw it this morning," she reminded the giant herbivore.

"Oh, yes, I remember now. I'll carry you there," offered the Diplodocus, stretching up his long neck. "Climb aboard and hang on tight."

Emma climbed onto the long neck and slid down it like a fireman sliding down his pole, coming to rest on the animal's broad back.

"Wait a minute, I'm coming with you," said the baby Gnathosaurus, sliding down beside her. "I've always wanted to go Far Away."

"But what'll your mother say?" asked Emma, doubtfully.

"She'll probably say "Good riddance to bad rubbish!" said the baby Gnathosaurus, screaming with laughter.

The Diplodocus set off clumping through the forest, with Emma and the baby Gnathosaurus clinging on tightly.

Conrad and Ivan, meanwhile, had searched far and wide for Emma, but could not find her anywhere. At length they sat down on a tree trunk, exhausted.

"I could bash that wretched Allosaurus on the nose," complained Ivan. "If it hadn't been for him, we wouldn't have lost her."

"The only thing we can do is get back to Belladonna," decided Conrad. "We must tell Lancelot the terrible news that Emma's lost."

"Come on then, we'd better make tracks," sighed Ivan, wearily.

Just as they got to their feet, there was a whistling noise and a noose dropped over their heads. It slipped down to their waists and tightened, tying them both together.

"Gotcher, you little beggars!" said a snarly voice, triumphantly. "Oh, 'is Lordship *is* going to be pleased with this catch."

The twins peered over their shoulders and there, holding the end of the lasso, was Throttlethumbs, grinning evilly, and looking twice as horrible as his photograph.

"Throttlethumbs!" gasped Conrad. "*Now* we're in trouble!"

"What's that? Trouble? With kind Throttlethumbs? No trouble—not unless you misbehave—and then I might twist your 'eads off and feed 'em to the dinosaurs," laughed Throttlethumbs, savagely.

The twins stood helpless while Throttlethumbs tied their hands behind their backs, giggling and humming as he did so.

"Now, young sirs," he announced at last, smacking his lips. "You're all tied up like a coupla Christmas turkeys. 'is Lordship *will* be pleased. Oh, yes! Now, forward march, young sirs, and don't dawdle, or I'll pull your hair out by the roots."

The twins stumbled through the forest followed by Throttlethumbs, who prodded them along with a thick stick he had found. Eventually, they came to the clearing where Jezabella was anchored, surrounded by the cages full of sobbing baby dinosaurs. Beneath a large, striped umbrella was a deck chair, and in it sat Sir Jasper, drinking champagne.

"Well, well," he drawled, peering at the twins through his

monocle. "What have we here? Lancelot's little helpers. That means the old bounder must be close by. How close, eh, boys? Tell me."

"You won't learn anything from us," responded Ivan, defiantly.

"Won't we?" sneered Sir Jasper. "We'll see if you don't change your tune after a few days of starvation and a few games with Throttlethumbs. He's not exactly gentle when he plays, you know."

"I certainly ain't," snarled Throttlethumbs, narrowing his eyes.

"Lock the boys in a cage," ordered Sir Jasper. "Then pack up quickly. If that old meddler Lancelot is hereabouts, we must move on to the Cretaceous period at once. Look sharp!"

Meanwhile, Emma and the baby Gnathosaurus, whom she had decided to call Albert, were nearing Belladonna after a very uncomfortable ride.

"Thank goodness you're safe," said Lancelot, as Emma slid down the Diplodocus's tail and landed at his feet.

"I'm fine," she said, "thanks to my friend. Where are the twins?"

"They've been captured by Throttlethumbs," explained Lancelot, "and imprisoned on Jezabella which has just taken off for the Cretaceous period. I saw it all through the telescope but I was too far away to help. We must follow at once. I dread to think what Sir Jasper may do to them. And that's not all. Your wretched Diplodocus egg has hatched and the baby has an appetite like a horse!"

Emma said good-bye to the Diplodocus and hurried after Lancelot into Belladonna.

As they climbed the stairs to the flight deck, he told her that although the baby was only the size of a corgi, her appetite was already immense.

"She's eaten half the orchard," he explained, as they strapped themselves into their seats. "She'll soon eat us out of house and home. Now, hang on tight. We must leave for the Cretaceous at once."

And with that he switched on the time machine.

CHAPTER FIVE

PRISONERS IN THE PAST

Lancelot and Emma had a very bumpy ride into the Cretaceous period. Belladonna burst through the time barrier with an enormous jerk that shook her from top to bottom. Lancelot banged his head on the controls and Emma hurt her elbow on the arm of her seat. There was a loud crash from the kitchen as crockery and glasses fell from the shelves and smashed on the floor.

They had arrived in the middle of a terrific thunderstorm. The plum-colored sky was split with jagged forks of lightning that crackled through the clouds. The rain fell in silver sheets that thumped on Belladonna like potatoes dropping on a drum. The thunder roared like a million cannons, nearly deafening them.

Since they could scarcely see a thing, it was no use looking for Jezabella and the twins. They anchored Belladonna and made tea. Emma made toast and gave a dozen apples to the baby Diplodocus, whom she christened Desdemona. Rather nervously, she offered Albert some sardines and was relieved when he decided that they were infinitely superior to octopus. In fact, it was only with the greatest difficulty that she managed to prevent him from eating the cans as well, since Albert thought that these were the shells. As he ate, he eyed Lancelot carefully.

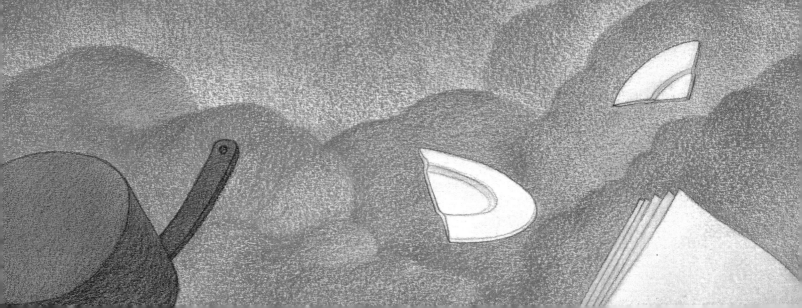

"Why are you so fat?" he asked, his beak full of sardines.

Lancelot choked on his tea, went as red as a lobster and had a coughing fit. When he had recovered, he glared at Albert.

"I am *not* fat," he insisted, "just a bit plump around the edges. And who are you to talk? You look like a bundle of old umbrellas."

"And you look as round as a turtle's egg," retorted Albert.

"Now, stop it, you two," interrupted Emma. "I think you're both beautiful. Lancelot, have another egg; and I know you'd like another can of sardines, Albert, wouldn't you?"

"Yum, yum, sardines." Albert clattered his beak with excitement as Emma opened a fresh can. "I could eat sardines till I burst."

"I wish you would," muttered Lancelot. Then, catching Emma's furious eye, he blushed and tried to seem innocent by humming a little tune.

Gradually, the thunder, lightning and rain ceased. When they eventually ventured out onto the flight deck the sky was as blue as a sapphire. Beautiful rainbows like multicolored croquet hoops stretched away as far as the eye could see.

"Now, this is where you can be useful for a change, instead of just guzzling sardines," Lancelot told Albert. "You know what a balloon is, don't you?"

"Yes, yes," said Albert, eagerly. "Beautiful Belladonna."

"Quite," sighed Lancelot. "Well, we want you to fly ahead and look for a balloon like Belladonna, only colored black and red.

Fly around and see what the humans with it are doing and then report back here. Do you understand?"

"Of course I understand," replied Albert. "I fly off and find a black-and-red Belladonna and ask the humans if they've got any sardines. They'll say yes, and I'll eat and eat until I burst."

"You won't do anything of the sort," shouted Lancelot. "You useless, leathery reptile. You'll find the balloon, see what the humans are doing and come straight back here. Is that understood?"

"Yes," confirmed Albert, nodding solemnly.

"When you get back, you shall have some sardines," promised Emma.

"Ah, that's more like it," said Albert, and launched himself off the side of the flight deck, with a great flapping of wings which blew Lancelot's hat off. Half an hour later he returned and landed.

"Not a sign of them," he reported. "I covered a huge area. I wheeled, I soared, I glided, I flapped, I zoomed, I banked, I . . ."

"Spare us the details," groaned Lancelot. "Where on earth can they have gone, I wonder?"

"Perhaps they've gone fishing for sardines," suggested Albert, looking hard at Emma. Taking the hint, she opened a new can for him.

"Oh, well, we'll just have to keep flying around and looking," sighed Lancelot. "It's the only thing we can do."

They flew along as fast as they could, helped by a stiff breeze which had sprung up. They came to a range of mountains, and as they flew over the upland meadows which were bright with flowers, they saw some most extraordinary dinosaurs.

The creatures stood on their hind legs, like giant kangaroos. The tops of their heads were armored with very thick bone, which made them look as though they were wearing crash helmets.

"They're pachycephalosaurs, also known as bone-heads," explained Lancelot. "It must be the mating season. Look over there."

A cluster of slender bone-heads, obviously females, their forepaws clasped together as if in prayer, stood by a group of rocks. They were making admiring noises while, nearby, two burly males circled around each other like boxers in a ring.

The males put their heads down and charged. They met with a great crash that echoed through the hills like a cannon shot. They backed away from each other, circled around and charged again. There was another terrific crash and all the female bone-heads

twittered and screamed with delight.

"Gracious! What a terrible noise!" complained Emma. "What on earth are they doing?"

"One of them is trying to win the other one's wives," Lancelot informed her. "They're having a duel to see which is the stronger. The winner will get the females. That's why they have that thick bone on their heads, to act like a battering ram."

"It seems a stupid way to behave," commented Emma. "I should think they'll both end up with terrible headaches."

"There are lots of animals in our own time which use their heads and horns for the same purpose," smiled Lancelot. "Deer and wild sheep do, for example, and so do buffaloes."

There was no time to linger and see the final outcome of the bone-heads' butting match, so they continued their flight over the mountains in search of Jezabella. On the other side of the peaks they found a huge cypress forest dotted with lakes. Emma, who was surveying the landscape through a telescope, was rewarded by seeing a flash of red in the trees.

"There's Jezabella," she cried, "over there to the west."

They landed out of sight by a large lake and Albert flew off on his second spying mission. He returned in a short while, very proud of himself.

"I've spotted four dinosaurs like you, only not so fat," he reported. "The two big ones have tied the two small ones to a tree."

"They must be using the twins as dinosaur bait," cried Emma.

"We must get there as quickly as we can," said Lancelot, putting on his coat. "Albert, you stay here on guard."

They made their way through the woods as fast as they could, but it was very marshy and they kept sinking up to their knees in mud.

"We'll never get there at this rate," gasped Lancelot.

"What's that enormous creature over there?" panted Emma.

Browsing placidly in the swamp ahead was a huge dinosaur with a body the size of an army tank. Its back was covered with jagged lumps which made it look like a gigantic, spiky tortoise.

"Scolosaurus," said Lancelot. "It's only got a brain the size of a walnut, and it's a harmless vegetarian. Maybe it'll give us a lift."

They waded up to the Scolosaurus, who was humming to himself.

"Excuse me," said Lancelot. "I wonder if you'd . . ."

"Aaaagh!" screamed the Scolosaurus, starting in alarm and rolling his eyes with terror. "Aaaagh! I give in. Don't hurt me."

"You stupid beast. How could *I* hurt you?" asked Lancelot.

"You're quite right," admitted the Scolosaurus, examining Lancelot and Emma. "You're much too small. What a relief!"

"We need to get through this swamp as quickly as possible. Would you carry us on your back?" asked Lancelot.

"I've never done anything like that before," he replied.

"We'll give you some delicious, juicy fruit," wheedled Emma.

"Fruit!" trumpeted Scolosaurus. "My favorite food! All right, I'll do it; but don't damage my spikes, stamping all over them."

As each of his horny spikes was the size of a small Christmas tree, there wasn't much chance of that, Emma thought, as they climbed up onto the Scolosaurus's back. Then, with Lancelot shouting instructions, they hung onto the dinosaur's bony spikes as he waddled, blundered and splashed his way through the swamp.

Their progress was slow, but at least it was quicker than wading through the mud. Eventually they reached the edge of the forest and, in the open ground ahead, they saw Jezabella. Nearby, the twins were tied to trees, while Sir Jasper was sitting in his deck chair, sipping champagne as usual.

"Now, you brats," he was saying to the twins, twirling his mustache. "I'm sure you'll be amused by the entertainment I'm providing for you. You're to be devoured by Tyrannosaurus Rex, King of the Dinosaurs. What an honor!"

He took a large, gold watch from his vest pocket and consulted it.

"The most fearsome of all dinosaurs should be along in about five minutes," he continued. "Throttlethumbs and I will go aloft in Jezabella to watch the fun, and *after* the monster has eaten you, I will shoot him and have his head stuffed to hang in my drawing room. When I get back to England, I shall be the most famous man in the whole world. I shall be hailed as the great dinosaur hunter, the conqueror of Tyrannosaurus and the inventor of the time machine."

"*You* didn't invent the time machine, Lancelot did," Ivan reminded him, angrily. "And anyway, you can't get back, you haven't got . . ."

"Shut up, Ivan," interrupted Conrad, quickly.

"What do you mean, I can't get back?" asked Sir Jasper, in an evil voice, screwing his monocle into his eye and glaring at Ivan.

"He didn't mean anything," replied Conrad, hurriedly.

"Do you want me to break both his legs and tear off his ears before he's eaten?" hissed Sir Jasper. "If you don't want that to happen to your brother, tell me what he meant . . ."

Conrad was trapped. He could not let his brother be tortured.

"You don't have a Gizmo," he said, reluctantly. "It's a vital part of the time machine. The time machine you stole brought you to the Age of Dinosaurs but, without a Gizmo, it can't get you back to our time."

"AAAAGH!" screamed Sir Jasper, in fury, throwing his bottle of champagne at Throttlethumbs and hitting him on the head. "Lancelot, the evil, hairy pumpkin! I might have known he had something like this up his sleeve."

Hidden in the bushes, Lancelot was delighted to see Sir Jasper's rage. He rocked with mirth and pushed his handkerchief into his mouth to stifle his laughter.

"Hee, hee," he chortled. "That'll learn him. That'll fix him. That'll teach him to . . ."

"Stop laughing," interrupted Emma, severely. "Now's the perfect time to rescue the twins. Sir Jasper hasn't got his gun, and Throttlethumbs is dazed by that bang on his head."

She rushed over to the Scolosaurus, and gabbled, "I want you to dash out over there and frighten those two away, so that we can rescue the ones tied to the trees."

"You'll have to say that more slowly," said the Scolosaurus, stupidly. "All these new ideas are giving me a headache. Start again and speak very clearly, please."

Although she was dying with impatience, Emma carefully repeated what she wanted the Scolosaurus to do.

"You're quite sure they won't hurt me?" he asked. "You see, I've got weak nerves, and any overexcitement, such as having a leg bitten off, could prove disastrous."

Emma assured him that neither Sir Jasper nor Throttlethumbs was capable of biting his leg off, so he took a deep breath and launched himself out of the bushes. He ran toward Sir Jasper, uttering a noise like a strangled sheep, which seemed to be his war cry. He did not sound very fearsome, but his appearance certainly had the desired effect. Taking one look at him thundering toward them, Sir Jasper and Throttlethumbs turned tail and ran off, as fast

as their legs could carry them, into the depths of the forest.

"I did it!" shouted the Scolosaurus, in surprise. "They ran away."

"Good for you," called Emma over her shoulder, as she and Lancelot rushed toward the twins and started cutting them loose.

"Thank goodness you're here," cried Conrad, in relief.

"We were just about to become lunch for a Tyrannosaurus," explained Ivan, who looked very pale.

"I know," panted Emma, sawing at the ropes. "We heard."

Just at that moment, there was a loud, thudding noise and the ground started to tremble. They heard a gargling roar, like a million knife grinders at work.

"Aaaagh," screamed the Scolosaurus, turning to run. "It's the monster, it's the monster! Oh, quick, quick, I must escape."

He started to run back the way they had come.

"Stop! Stop!" shouted Emma. "You must take us with you."

"Well, hurry up," he shrieked, "or we'll all be eaten!"

As they hacked desperately at the ropes binding the twins, Tyrannosaurus Rex burst into view.

CHAPTER SIX

TROUBLE WITH TYRANNOSAURUS

The monstrous horror stopped at the edge of the clearing. Conrad's mouth fell open and Emma's knees turned to water. The creature was as tall as a house and his head was as big as a car. As he opened his jaws to give a terrifying roar, Emma saw a glittering array of teeth, each as long as a carving knife and dripping with saliva. His titanic body was supported on two immensely powerful hind legs armed with enormous talons. His ridiculously tiny front legs ended in claws like curved daggers.

The Tyrannosaurus fixed the children with his cold, merciless eyes and began to stalk purposefully toward them. The ground shook with each giant footstep.

"Oh, quick, quick!" screamed Emma, in panic. "Faster!"

The final rope parted, not a moment too soon! They raced toward the trembling Scolosaurus and scrambled up onto his back. The Scolosaurus started to waddle toward the trees as fast as he could but the Tyrannosaurus, which took huge strides like a giant in seven-league boots, soon caught up.

They cowered down on the Scolosaurus's back. The terrifying Tyrannosaurus loomed over them, gazing down with blazing, black eyes, his jaws gaping wide. Then a curious thing happened.

Spurred on by terror, the Scolosaurus unexpectedly swung his powerful tail.

"Hold on tight!" he yelled to the children.

They watched, open-mouthed, as the bone club on the end of the Scolosaurus's tail crashed into the Tyrannosaurus's legs. The monster screamed with pain.

"Take that, and that and that," shrieked the Scolosaurus, lashing his tail wildly. "And *that!* I'm sick of you, you great bully!"

"That's unfair. It's a foul," roared the Tyrannosaurus, in agony. "You're not supposed to fight back. *I'm* the king."

While the Tyrannosaurus staggered about moaning, blood pouring from his legs, the Scolosaurus, with a remarkable turn of speed, dashed into the forest. Being built like a tank, he just crashed through the trees, whereas the Tyrannosaurus, who was taller, soon got tangled up in the branches and was left far behind.

They reached the clearing where their
balloons were anchored.

"Hooray! You're back," squeaked Desdemona.
"Can I have an apple?"

"I must say, a sardine wouldn't go amiss,"
murmured Albert.

"You animals only seem to think about your
stomachs," said Emma, severely, collecting
a basket of apples and carrying it out to
where Lancelot was deep in conversation
with the Scolosaurus.

"Look," Lancelot was suggesting to him,
"if *we* get rid of Tyrannosaurus for *you*,
can *you* help *us* to get rid of Sir Jasper?"

"I'd be delighted to help," he replied.

"Bring your friends and relatives here
at dawn," Lancelot instructed him.

"Here's the fruit we promised," said
Emma, presenting the basket.

"Goodness! How beautiful it looks,"
drooled the Scolosaurus in delight,
gobbling up not only the apples but
the basket as well.

"Now," announced Lancelot, when the Scolosaurus had waddled off, well satisfied. "We've got to catch that awful Tyrannosaurus and then put Jezabella out of action, so we can capture Sir Jasper. What we need is an air attack. Albert, you go and find as many pterosaurs as you can and bring them back here. While you're doing that, we'll deal with the Tyrannosaurus."

Albert flew away. Lancelot and the children found their thickest, strongest silk ropes and filled two dustbins full of sand.

They took off in search of their quarry. The twins traveled in Minidonna, Emma and Lancelot in Belladonna. Presently they reached open grassland and were skimming along at a good rate.

"What are those animals standing in a circle?" shouted Ivan, who was lookout.

"Ceratopsians," replied Lancelot. "They'd be wonderful allies in our attack on Sir Jasper. Let's drop down and enlist their help."

The ceratopsians looked like huge rhinos, but with long, heavy tails. They each had a fan of spikes around their necks and three enormous horns on their noses. The adults were standing in a protective circle with their young in the middle.

"Those terrible horns should frighten Sir Jasper," said Ivan, hugging himself with glee.

Lancelot explained the situation to the ceratopsians, who readily agreed to help.

"Come to the lake in the cypress forest tomorrow at dawn," called Lancelot, as Belladonna sailed aloft again.

They flew over the ridge and came upon an astonishing sight.

In the valley was a huge dinosaur nursery where hundreds of duck-billed lambeosaurs had built their nests. These were as big as bathtubs and packed together so the parents could sing and gossip to one another while they waited for their eggs to hatch.

The adults had long necks and tails, and on their heads were extraordinary horns shaped like hatchet blades. Behind each crest was a straight spike. As they sat on their nests chattering to each other through their flabby beaks, their shrill voices sounded like a million piccolos piping.

Without warning, the Tyrannosaurus appeared over the hill. As soon as they saw him, the duckbills screamed and fled in every direction. The Tyrannosaurus strode through the abandoned nests, dipping his horrific face into them as though they were bowls of soup. His jaws were soon yellow and dripping with egg yolk, and his mouth was full of wriggling, squeaking, baby duckbills.

"Quick," shouted Lancelot. "Action stations!"

Minidonna flew to one side of the Tyrannosaurus as Belladonna flew to the other. Lancelot, Emma and the twins had their nooses and dustbins at the ready. The Tyrannosaurus looked up and recognized them. He opened his mouth with a roar of fury.

"Dustbins away!" ordered Lancelot, loudly.

Emma and Conrad emptied their dustbins directly on top of the Tyrannosaurus's head, filling his great mouth and his glittering eyes with sand. The huge creature, blinded, screamed with rage and blundered about in circles, shaking his head violently. Lancelot and Ivan managed to get a noose around each of the giant animal's forelegs. Emma, with a lucky throw, got one around his massive jaws and Conrad got one around his tail.

"Now, haul away," called Lancelot.

Emma and Conrad started the winches. In next to no time, the Tyrannosaurus was hoisted aloft, bound, blinded and helpless. He moaned and roared with rage as he twirled round and round.

"Listen, you duckbills," Lancelot called down. "We've got rid of one terrible enemy, but you're all still in great danger from an even worse creature. Come to the lake in the cypress forest tomorrow at dawn and we'll tell you how you can save yourselves."

"We will, we promise," twittered the duckbills. They all cheered as Belladonna sped away, carrying the Tyrannosaurus with her.

Lancelot and the children flew several miles to a very long, deep canyon and dropped the Tyrannosaurus into a shallow lake.

"That'll keep him out of the way," said Lancelot with satisfaction. "There are plenty of fish, so he won't starve. Now back to the lake for a well-earned rest before tomorrow's attack."

CHAPTER SEVEN

THE REVENGE OF THE DINOSAURS

Just before dawn the next day, as they were having breakfast, Lancelot and the children heard a great whooshing, swishing noise, like a hurricane. Rushing outside and squinting into the rising sun, they saw Albert flying over the trees. Behind him, their wings beating the cool morning air, were twenty enormous pterosaurs. Each had a wingspan as big as a glider, and a very long, pointed beak.

"Hello, everyone," said Albert, as he landed on the flight deck. "What do you think of my friends, eh? Pretty nifty bunch, aren't they? I think they'll fix old Sir Jasper, don't you?"

"Great heavens! They're quetzalcoatls, the biggest of all the pterosaurs," gasped Lancelot, as the huge beasts landed in a rather ungainly manner with a great crackling of wings.

"We've got our own prehistoric air force," laughed Ivan.

"It's just what we need. You *are* clever, Albert," said Emma, and Albert looked down modestly.

"Excellent," said Lancelot, rubbing his hands. "Now, here's my plan. When the rest of our forces arrive, Albert will lead the quetzalcoatls to Sir Jasper's camp. They'll dive-bomb—I'm sorry, I mean dive-puncture—Jezabella and immobilize her. While that's going on, we'll surround the camp and then we'll have him. He'll have no choice but to surrender. How's that for genius?"

"Full marks!" cheered the twins. "Excellent!"

"Can I lead the air force?" asked Emma. "I could ride on Albert."

"Well . . . all right," conceded Lancelot, reluctantly, "but it's a tricky business and you mustn't take any risks."

"I'll look after her," Albert reassured him.

So it was arranged, and they settled down to wait for the other dinosaurs. Before long, the ground shook with the tread of massive feet. All the other dinosaurs who had promised to come were there, and a few more besides. There were fifty duckbills, their old friend the Scolosaurus, and twenty of his relatives called ankylosaurs. They were just as big as he and looked like armadillos covered

with sharp spikes. There were about sixty ceratopsians too, their horns looking very warlike in the pale, dawn light.

Lancelot made a speech explaining about Sir Jasper and what he was doing. There was a howl of rage from the audience. He then explained his plan of campaign. The dinosaurs roared in approval.

The ground force set off—Conrad and Ivan riding very big ceratopsians, and Lancelot perched on the back of the Scolosaurus. Meanwhile, Emma gave Albert silk reins to hold in his beak, so she could guide him.

"Stay here," she told Desdemona. "I'll give you some apples when we get back."

Desdemona didn't know whether to be sad because Emma was going, or happy that she would soon have some apples. Emma patted the confused Desdemona good-bye and climbed onto Albert's back. Gripping him firmly with her knees, she took hold of the reins and cried, "Off we go, Albert."

As Albert flapped his way higher and higher, Emma felt a great surge of excitement. The squadron of quetzalcoatls flew behind them, filling the air with the swishing of their wings.

"Higher, Albert, higher," shouted Emma.

Up they flew, the wind buffeting them, until they were so high that the ponds and marshes below looked like bits of broken mirrors glittering in the sun's rays.

"How do you like it?" called Albert.

"Fantastic!" Emma shouted. "Simply wonderful. I wouldn't have missed this for anything."

From her great height, Emma had a wonderful view. She followed the progress of the dinosaur horde with her telescope.

Lancelot led the dinosaurs to the edge of the clearing in which Sir Jasper had made his camp. Then he signaled to them to spread out in a circle. Soon, a solid mass of dinosaurs—a fearsome wall of horns, spikes and teeth—surrounded Jezabella and the campsite. When they were all in position, Lancelot waved his hat and gazed up high into the sky where the prehistoric air force circled. When Emma saw Lancelot wave, she shouted,

"Right, Albert, there's the signal! Off we go!"

"Wheeee!" cried Albert, putting his head down and going into a steep nose dive.

Unwisely, Emma had dropped the reins while she looked through her telescope. When Albert went into his nose dive, she was quite unprepared and had nothing to hold onto. The speed of the dive created such a sudden, rushing wind that Emma was swept straight off Albert's back and fell head over heels through the sky.

Emma was terrified as she tumbled through the air. The sky was below her one second and above her the next. Her ears were filled with the roaring of the wind, but she could just hear Albert.

"It's all right, Emma. It's all right," came his faint cries.

"It's all very well for *him* to say it's all right," she thought. "*He's* got wings."

Albert shouted to one of the quetzalcoatls to swoop down and fly beneath Emma. She fell onto one of its great wings and bounced as if she were on a trampoline. Grabbing hold of the thick fur, she hung on grimly. Presently, Albert landed on the wing next to her.

"Steady," protested the quetzalcoatl. "You're making me fly all lopsided."

"Sorry," panted Albert. "Shan't be a minute. Now, Emma, get on my back again. Can't have you flying about without wings. That would put us pterosaurs out of a job."

Emma scrambled back onto him and took a firm grip of the reins. Off they went again, zooming down toward Jezabella.

"Pterosaurs!" shouted Albert, aiming
himself like a guided missile at Jezabella.
"Do your duty. Plunge to puncture!"
Albert swooped straight down on top of the
balloon, stuck his beak in as deeply as he could,
then withdrew it. There was a sharp, hissing sound
as the air started to escape. Then the quetzalcoatls,
banking on their wide wings, dived at the stricken
balloon. There were loud pops and hisses as each pterosaur
punctured the silk, zoomed around and came in for another attack.
In next to no time, the balloon crumpled and collapsed. One
corner started to ripple and flap as Sir Jasper and Throttlethumbs
fought their way through the swathes of silk, finally emerging
red-faced and panting on Jezabella's flight deck.

"What's going on?" shouted Sir Jasper, in a fury. "Who has had
the audacity to destroy my precious Jezabella?"

"Us!" roared Lancelot, triumphantly, gesturing at his army.

Looking around, Sir Jasper saw, for the first time, the sea of angry
dinosaurs that surrounded him.

THE REVENGE OF THE DINOSAURS

"Lancelot! You devil!" yelled Sir Jasper, hopping about in rage.

"Your balloon is grounded," shouted Lancelot, "and you can't kill all these dinosaurs. Surrender, or be trampled to death!"

Throttlethumbs handed Sir Jasper his big gun.

"Aha!" snarled Sir Jasper, taking aim. "I may not be able to kill all the dinosaurs, but I can put an end to one meddling old fool."

"Quick, quick," said Emma to Albert. "Do something!"

Albert swooped, Sir Jasper fired and Lancelot reeled back. He slid off the Scolosaurus onto the ground. Then Albert, too late, wrenched the gun from Sir Jasper's grasp.

"Oh, quick, take me to Lancelot," cried Emma, in desperation.

Albert set off, dropping the gun at Conrad's feet as he flew past the twins. Conrad snatched it up and kept Sir Jasper and Throttlethumbs covered. Emma slipped from Albert's back and ran through the forest of dinosaur legs to where Lancelot lay.

"Lancelot! Are you all right?" cried Emma, kneeling beside him.

"Yes," he groaned. "It's painful, but it's only a flesh wound."

"Is he dead?" asked Ivan, horrified by all the blood.

"Takes more than a Collywobble to kill me," Lancelot answered, grimly. "But you must stop the bleeding. Ivan and Conrad, go and tie up those two crooks and then find their medicine chest."

The twins ran off, while Emma cut away Lancelot's shirt with her penknife. The bullet had gone straight through his shoulder, leaving a clean wound. Lancelot moved his arm, experimentally.

"No bones broken, thank goodness," he winced. "It'll soon heal. Be as right as rain in next to no time."

Ivan and Conrad came back with the medicine chest, and Emma busied herself fixing Lancelot's wound.

"We tied each of the villains to a dinosaur's leg," reported Conrad. "They'll be knelt on if they give any trouble."

"They were terribly scared," laughed Ivan. "Throttlethumbs went so white he looked as if he'd taken a bath."

"Excellent," said Lancelot. "That'll do nicely, Emma dear. A most comfortable sling. Thank you. Now we have much to do."

Lancelot stood up and, although he swayed a bit, managed to make his way to Sir Jasper's deck chair where he sat down heavily.

"Now," he commanded, "bring those villains here to me."

The two of them looked pretty silly—Sir Jasper in his striped pajamas, and Throttlethumbs in his ridiculous nightshirt and nightcap. Lancelot gazed at them gravely.

"You really are an evil pair," he announced in an accusing voice. "You've killed several innocent dinosaurs, captured their babies, kidnapped the twins and attempted to murder me."

"I can explain that, dear old Lancelot," wheedled Sir Jasper, smiling at Lancelot as if he were his best friend. "The gun went off by accident. It just happened to be pointing in your direction. A pure and simple accident, my dear fellow."

"You liar!" shouted Emma. "I saw you aiming the gun."

"Yes, and Throttlethumbs brought him the gun, so he's equally to blame," added Conrad, angrily.

"We ought to go and put them in the lake with that beastly Tyrannosaurus," said Ivan. "That would serve them right."

"No, no, not that," begged Throttlethumbs, falling to his knees. "Not Tyranno . . . thing. Oh, no, please, kind young master, have pity on poor Throttlethumbs what never did any 'arm to no one."

"No, we'll take them back to face justice," decided Lancelot. "For the present we'll put them on a diet of bread and water and make them work for it. They can start by bathing all the baby dinosaurs before we take them back to their families."

Lancelot thanked the dinosaurs for their help and said that he hoped they would now be able to live in peace again. The baby dinosaurs, when told that they were going back to their families, were, of course, quite overjoyed. They screamed, shouted and sang loudly. The noise gave Lancelot a splitting headache.

"If you don't all shut up," he shouted, irritably, "we won't take you back to your families at all!"

The babies fell silent and started to line up for their baths. Sir Jasper was provided with a long hose, Throttlethumbs was given a large scrubbing brush and several bars of scented soap, and they set to work.

The air rang with cries like, "Now don't get soap in my eye or I'll bite you!"

"Scrub my back again, will you?"

"A little more suds in my armpit, please."

The babies thought being bathed was such good fun that, as soon as they had finished, they rejoined the line for another turn. Conrad and Ivan identified all the baby dinosaurs and tied big labels around their necks, saying "Triassic" or "Jurassic" or "Cretaceous." Lancelot left them to it and went off into the forest with his film camera.

It took them a week, with the aid of Belladonna and Minidonna, to get all the baby dinosaurs back to their correct periods in time, but at length it was done. Then it was time to leave.

"Don't you want to go back to your family?" Emma asked Desdemona for the umpteenth time.

"No, Mama, please let me stay with you," she pleaded.

"I'd *much* rather stay with you. I want to be with you forever."

"Wouldn't it be nicer to be with your family?" persisted Emma.

"They'd just steal my apples," retorted Desdemona.

"We'll go to Far Away together," crowed Albert. "What a lark!"

The spiders had done a magnificent job repairing the holes in Jezabella. She floated beside Belladonna, tethered securely to the bamboo house. Sir Jasper and Throttlethumbs, exhausted after bathing all the baby dinosaurs, were safely chained in their own cages. Everything was ready for departure.

The dinosaurs reassembled to see them off. All the babies stood in the front row, howling tearfully. The children said good-bye and waved until they thought their arms would drop off. Then, leading Albert and Desdemona, they made their way to the flight deck and strapped themselves into their seats.

Lancelot pressed the button. There was a bang, a whoosh, a swoosh and a flash of rainbow-colored lights. Before the astonished gaze of the dinosaurs, Belladonna, Minidonna and Jezabella simply vanished into the air like burst soap bubbles.

The dinosaurs looked disbelievingly at the spot where their friends had been. Sobbing sadly, they turned away, then waddled, slithered, lumbered and flapped their way back to their swamps, forests and grasslands.

POSTSCRIPT

After a long flight full of bumps, squeaks, flashes, roars and bangs owing to the extra weight of Jezabella, they arrived back at the Dollybutt cottage. Here, after they had greeted Mrs. Dollybutt and revived her (for she had fainted at the sight of Desdemona and Albert), they phoned the local police. Four large constables and a fierce-looking sergeant marched Sir Jasper and Throttlethumbs away to the police station. They were charged with attempted murder, robbery and dinosaur rustling.

The judge gave them ten years' imprisonment in the worst prison in the realm, Festering Castle. Here, on a lonely island off the Scottish coast, they were fed on sago, carrots, bread and water. They spent their days breaking huge rocks up into little pebbles. After some years they managed to escape, disguised as Highland cattle, and caused a lot of trouble. But that's another story. . . .

The Dollybutt cottage became a hive of activity while they all got ready for the day when Lancelot would give his lecture to the Royal Zoological Society at the Albert Hall. The lecture, accompanied by the films Lancelot had taken, was entitled "Dinosaurs past and present." The children were sure it would be a sensation.

Mrs. Dollybutt made Lancelot a handsome velvet dinner jacket and a lace-fronted shirt. Emma had a new dress, the twins had new suits, while Desdemona and Albert just had baths. Albert agreed to have a bath (as he was frightened his wings would shrink) only when Emma told him that the lecture was to take place in a huge hall named after him.

Rumors leaked out that Lancelot was going to show a film of real dinosaurs which he had obtained under mysterious circumstances. The telephone in the cottage rang constantly as reporters from leading newspapers and magazines tried to discover if this were true. Lancelot just told them to wait and see.

The reporters then asked leading scientists for their opinions and they replied it was a load of nonsense. " 'Real dinosaurs are piffle,' says Professor," announced one newspaper headline. " 'Lancelot is loopy,' says well-known expert," pronounced another. The children were furious, and so was Albert, who was most insulted by being described as piffle, after he was told what it meant. Lancelot merely smiled and said, "Wait for the night."

91

The great night came. Desdemona and Albert, who had been kept out of sight in the barn all this time, were smuggled to the Albert Hall in a big truck before anyone else arrived. Emma and Albert were concealed on stage in a large box, while the twins were hidden behind the scenery with Desdemona and a pile of apples.

The audience started to arrive. The press and television were there, and so were all the great scientists of the day, led by Professor Porteous Pigglestrotter, the world's foremost expert on dinosaurs. All had come to see Lancelot make a fool of himself. None of them believed the rumors about a time machine and real dinosaurs.

Lancelot walked onto the stage to cries of "Boo!" and "Liar!" He took no notice, but waited for silence and then began his lecture.

His talk about the time machine and their adventure was greeted with loud laughter. He ignored this. Finally, he showed the film he had taken of the dinosaurs.

"It's a fake!" cried several voices in the audience.

When the film was over, Professor Pigglestrotter climbed on stage and held up his hand for silence.

"We all enjoyed watching your charming fairy tale," he sneered. "Perhaps you'd tell us how you faked your monsters."

"All right, if you don't believe me or my film, maybe you'll believe the evidence of your own eyes. Emma! Twins!" Lancelot roared. "Action stations!"

The twins led Desdemona onto the stage. There was an uproar! Albert soared up to the roof and dived, zooming across the orchestra pit and out over the heads of the audience. Pandemonium reigned!

Professor Pigglestrotter uttered a cry of terror, stepped backward, and fell off the stage. As Albert whizzed low over the heads of the audience, half the people tried to hide under their seats and the other half fainted. It was a long time before order was restored, and it took a stream of ambulances to ferry all those with black eyes and bruises to the hospital.

Of course, the next day, the press was full of it. "Lancelot, King of the Dinosaurs," shouted one headline. "Dinosaurs alive and well," screamed another. There were photographs of Lancelot and the children with Albert and Desdemona.

They were even invited to appear on television.

"Do you intend to market your extraordinary machine?" asked the TV interviewer.

"No," replied Lancelot, firmly. "Tourists are ill-mannered enough in this day and age. I'm not going to have them trampling about all over history, leaving their rubbish around and spoiling it for others. One day, maybe, when people are better behaved."

Both Desdemona and Albert got very good contracts to star in TV commercials. Desdemona was shown munching away at a huge pile of apples, wearing a badge saying, "A Granny Smith a day keeps Tyrannosaurus Rex away." Albert was shown diving into the sea off Bournemouth, emerging from the sea with a can of sardines on which was written, "I always eat Smith and Snaith's smooth, silvery, slippery sardines." These TV appearances kept them well supplied with apples and sardines, as you can imagine. In addition to this, a palatial new home was built for them behind the cottage. A sign on top said, "Delamay's Dutch Barns, designed for Desdemona Dinosaur."

"Well," said Lancelot, when all the fuss and hoo-ha had died down a little, "who'd have thought that a little journey in time would create such a sensation?"

"But it *was* sensational!" the children chorused, and then fell silent, looking wistfully at Lancelot.

"You know," mused Lancelot, after a deliberate pause, "it does seem rather a shame to let Belladonna, Minidonna and the time machine gather cobwebs."

"You mean . . ." said Emma, slowly, hardly daring to believe her ears, ". . . you mean we could go on another trip?"

"Why not?" replied Lancelot. "But only if you're sure you want to, of course," he added mischievously.

You may be sure the children left him in no doubt about that!